D0776362

SOMETHING NEW TO DO

Written by Ski Michaels
Illustrated by Jan Palmer

Troll Associates

Library of Congress Cataloging in Publication Data

—

Something new to do.

Summary: Constantly in search of new things to do, a young octopus has some scary experiences.
[1. Octopus—Fiction. 2. Marine animals—Fiction]
I. Palmer, Jan, ill. II. Title.
PZ7.P3656SO 1986 [E] 85-14021
ISBN 0-8167-0634-4 (lib. bdg.)
ISBN 0-8167-0635-2 (pbk.)

Copyright © 1986 by Troll Associates
All rights reserved. No part of this book may be used or reproduced in any manner whatsoever without written permission from the publisher.
Printed in the United States of America

10 9 8 7 6 5 4

SOMETHING NEW TO DO

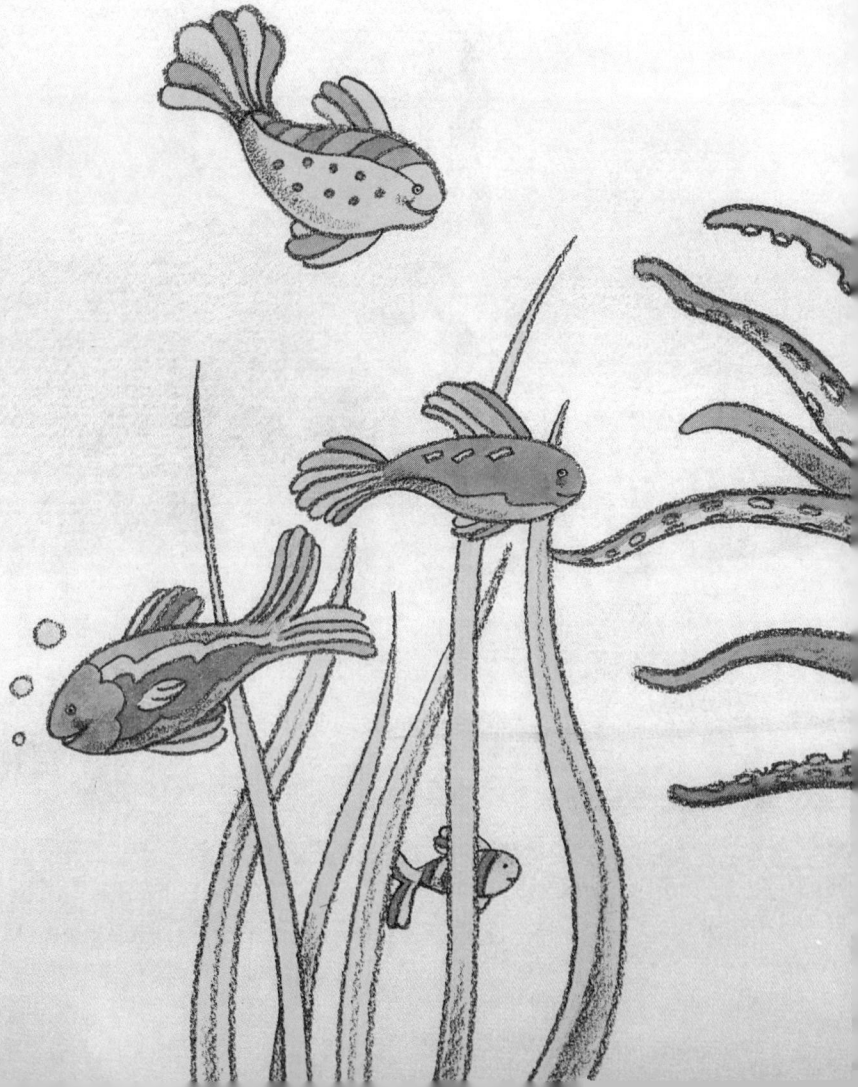

Elroy was special. He had eight long, wiggly arms. His arms had a special name. They were called "tentacles." Elroy was an octopus.

The ocean was Elroy's home. There were lots of things to do in the ocean. It was a fun place to live.

He went swimming. Swimming was fun.

He went fishing. Fishing was fun.

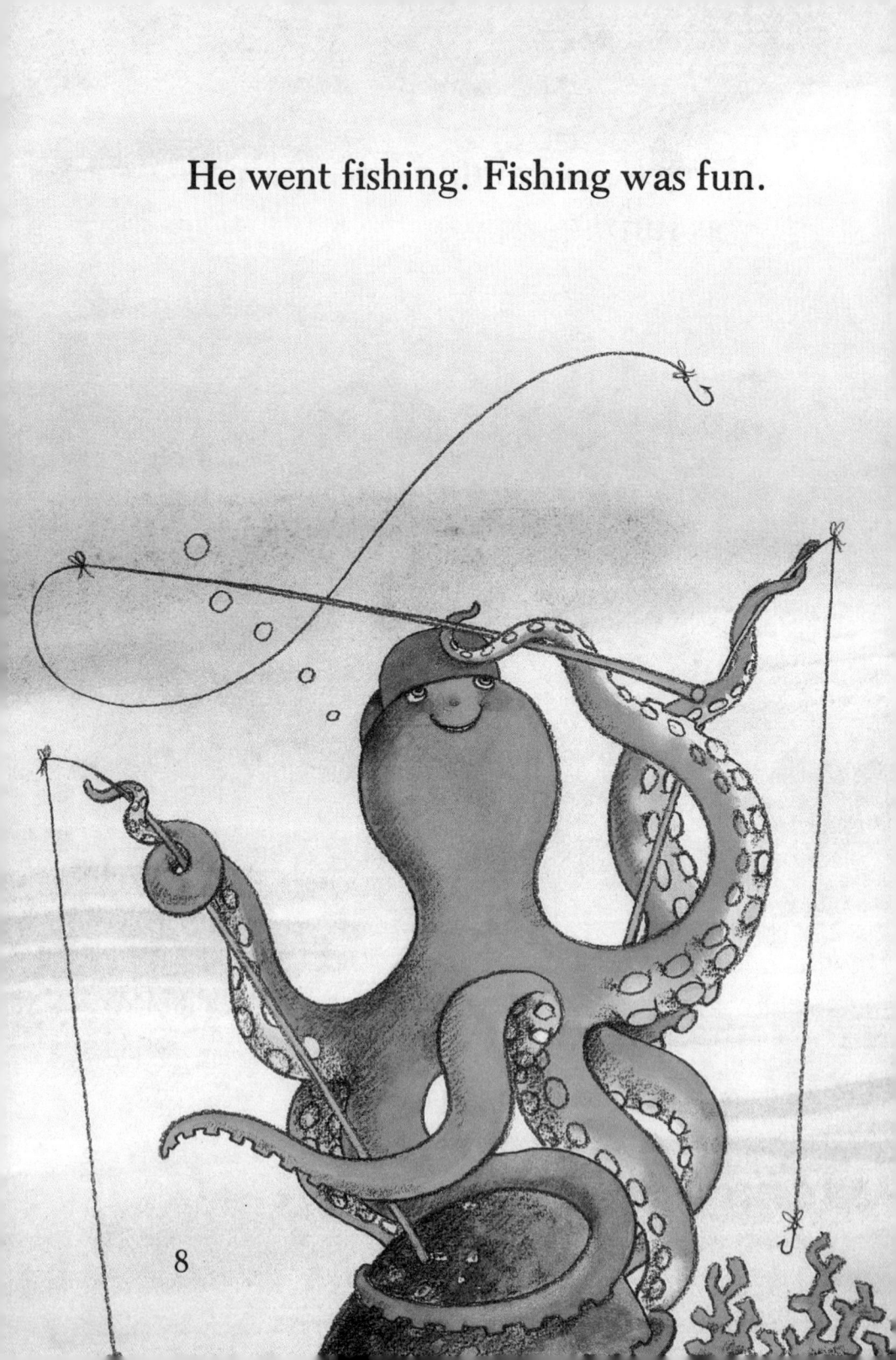

Often he sat on a big, black rock and juggled shells. Juggling was fun. But sometimes while juggling, his tentacles got all tangled up. His arms ended up in knots. What a mess!

It took hours to untangle his arms and untie the knots. Poor, poor Elroy.

One day Elroy said, "I'm tired of swimming. I'm tired of fishing. I'm tired of juggling. I need something new to do."
Off he went to do something new.

After awhile he saw something new. It was buried in the sand. "What is that?" Elroy asked.

"To find out I must dig," he said. "Digging in the sand is something new to do."
So dig he did.

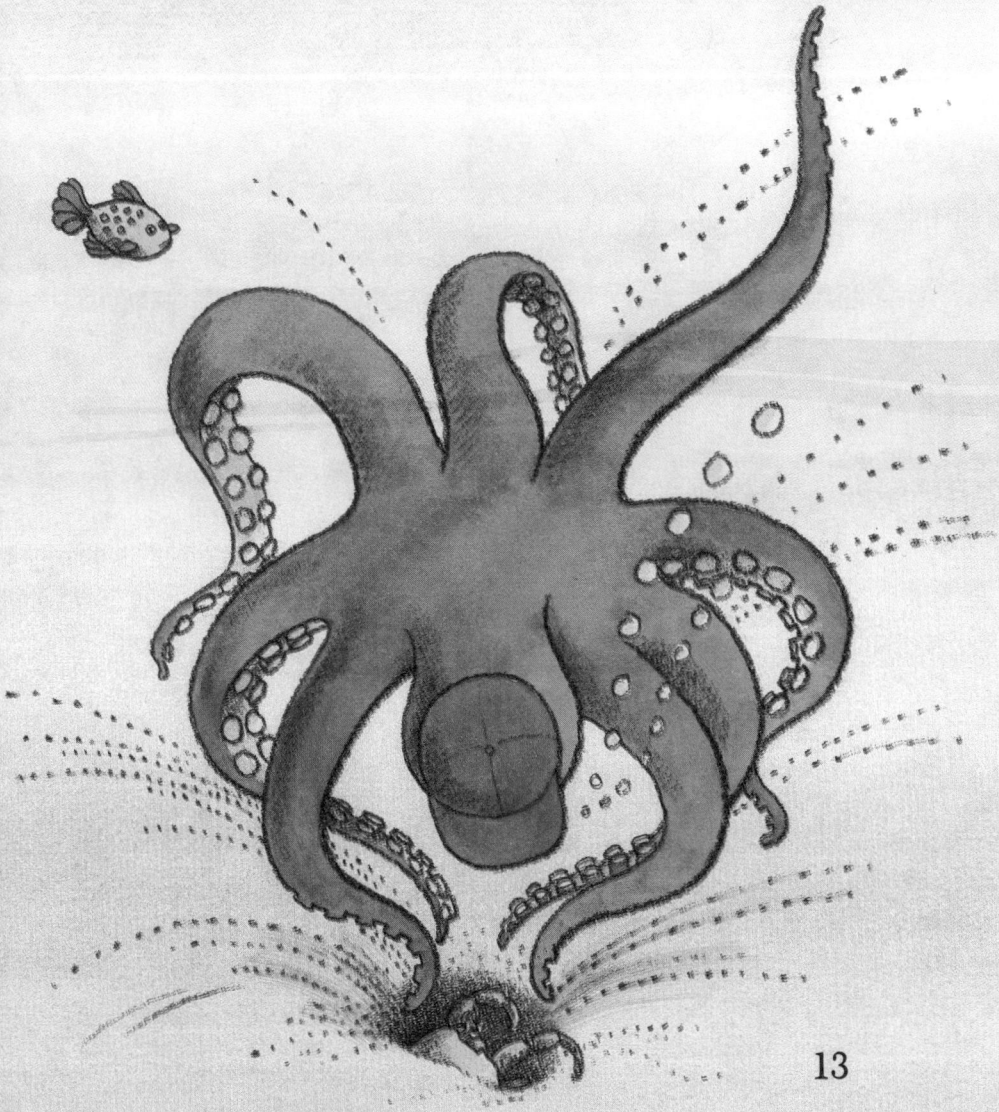

Elroy dug up the new thing. But the new thing did not want to be dug up. It wanted to stay buried in the sand.

The thing was a hermit crab. It wanted to be left alone. A hermit crab is not very friendly.

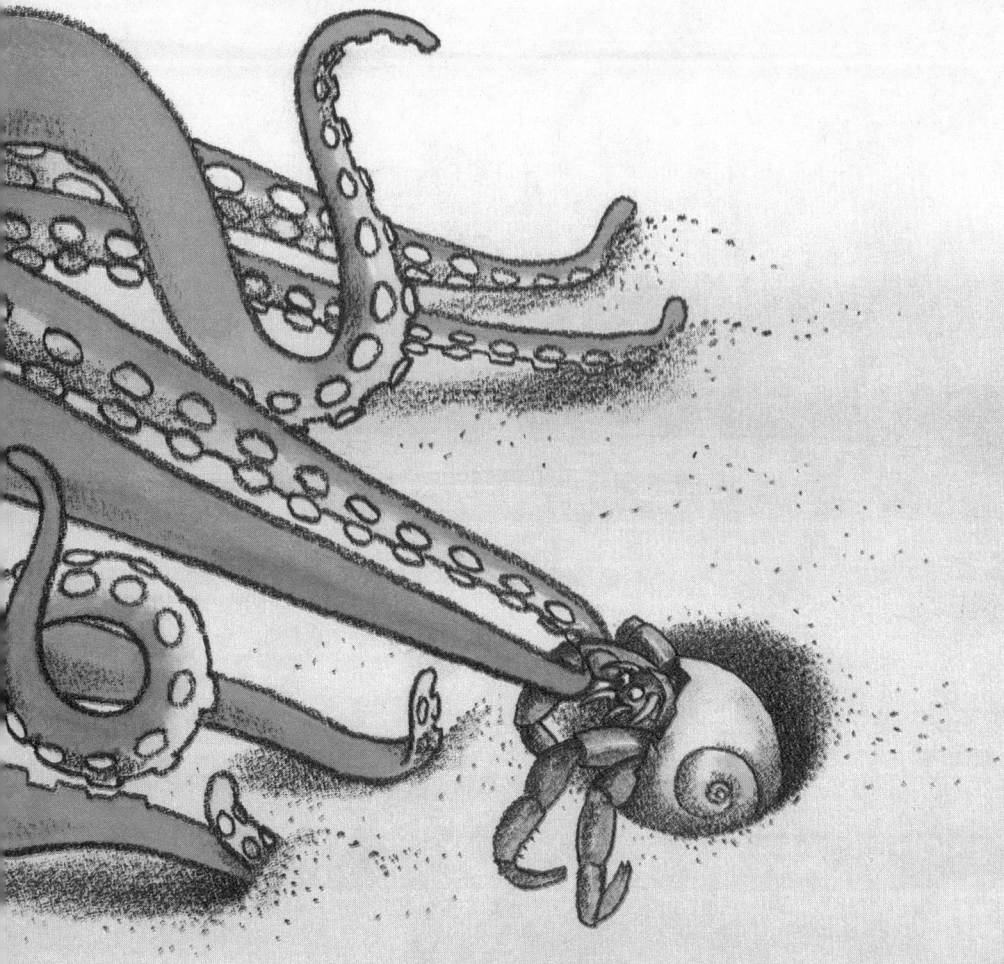

"This is fun," said Elroy.
"This is not fun," cried the
hermit crab.
The hermit crab pinched Elroy.

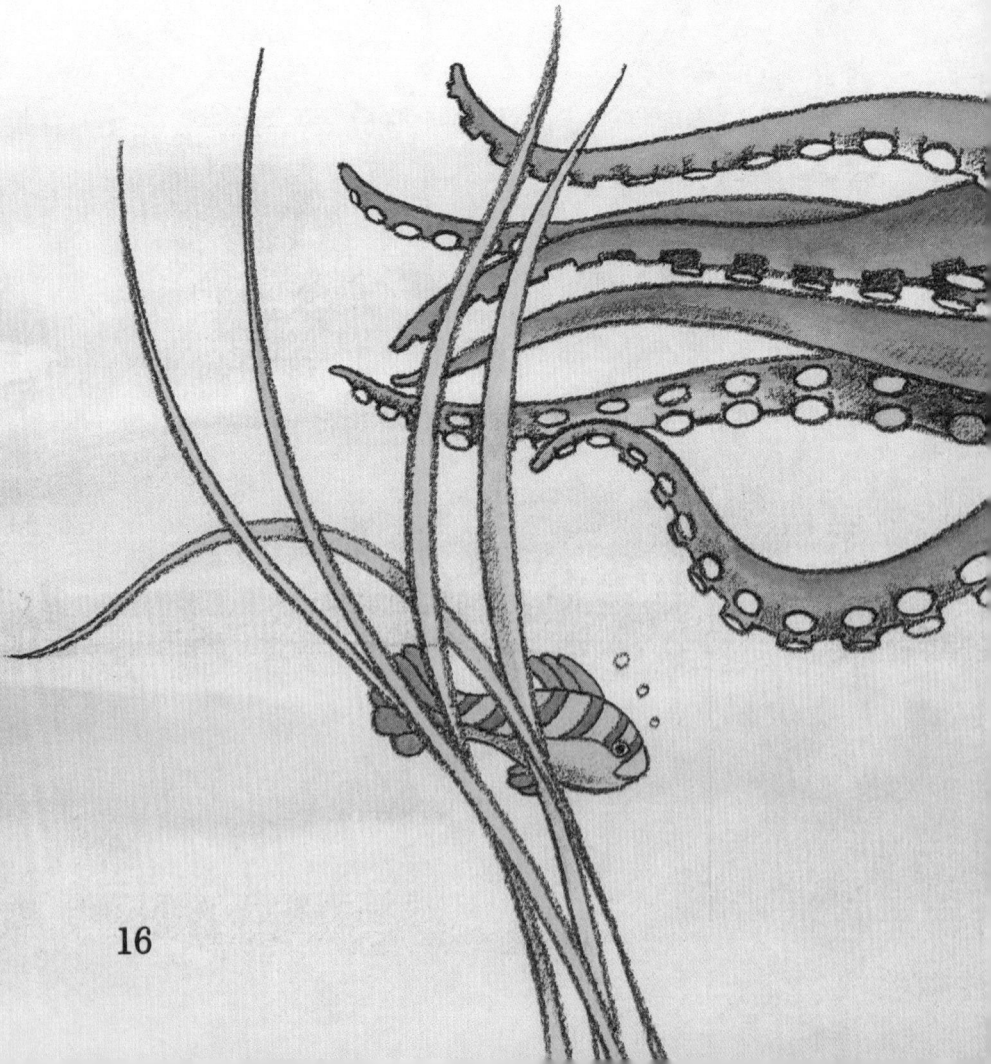

"Ouch," cried Elroy. "Getting pinched is not fun at all!"

Elroy left the hermit crab alone.
"I want something new to do
that does not pinch," said Elroy.
So away he went.

Elroy swam this way. Nothing new there. Elroy swam that way. Nothing new there.

He swam every which way.
It was not easy to find something
new to do.

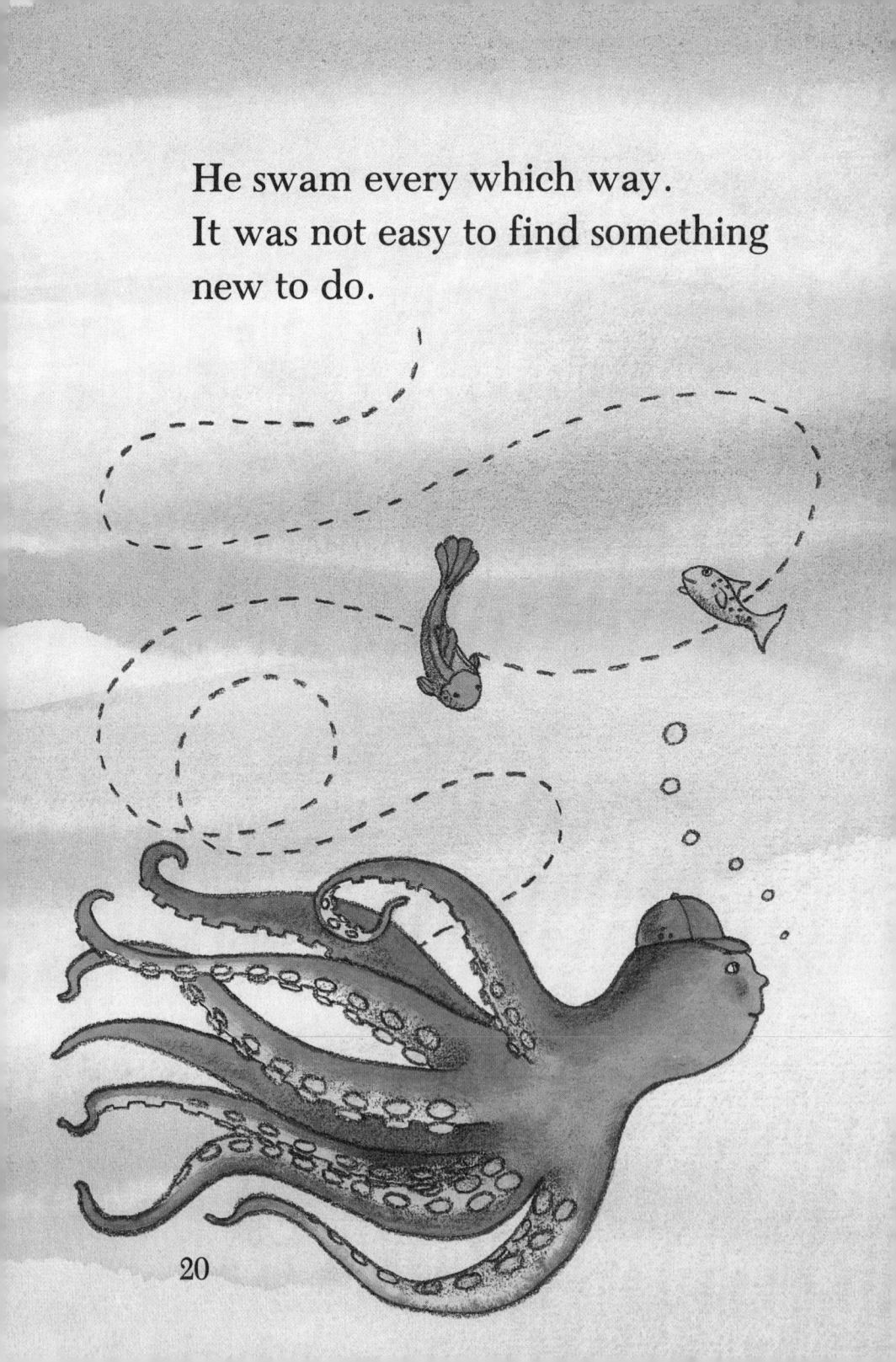

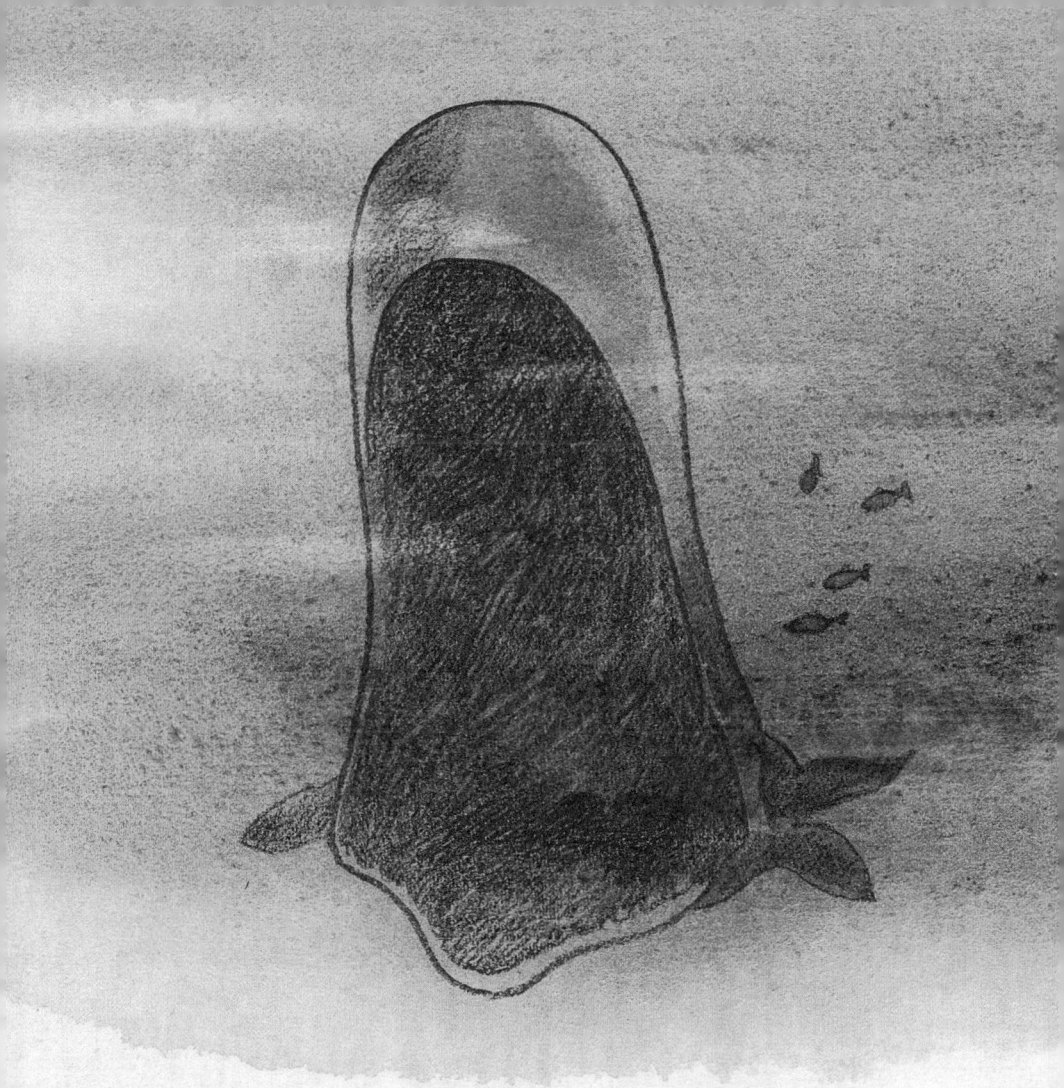

"There is something," cried Elroy, "something new. It is big. It is dark. I think it is the big, dark mouth of a cave. I like caves!"

Elroy swam in. He swam into the mouth of the big, dark cave.

"This cave looks funny," said Elroy. "It has teeth. It has a big tongue. *Yipes!* This is not a cave! It is the mouth of a whale."

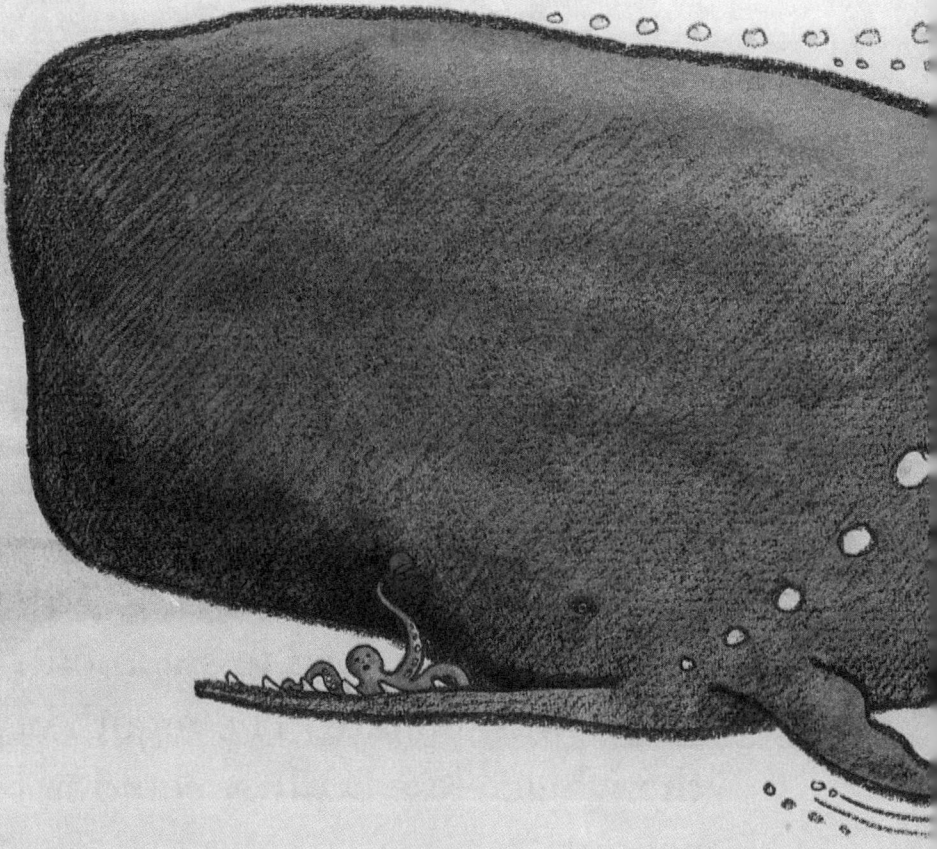

Quickly, Elroy tried to swim out. But it was too late. The mouth of the whale closed. Elroy could not get out.

"Help! Help! Help!" Elroy yelled.
His yells made bubbles. The bubbles tickled the whale's tongue.

"Ah-choo!" sneezed the whale. Out came Elroy. Out he came very fast! The sneeze sent him spinning top over tentacles. Around and around he went.

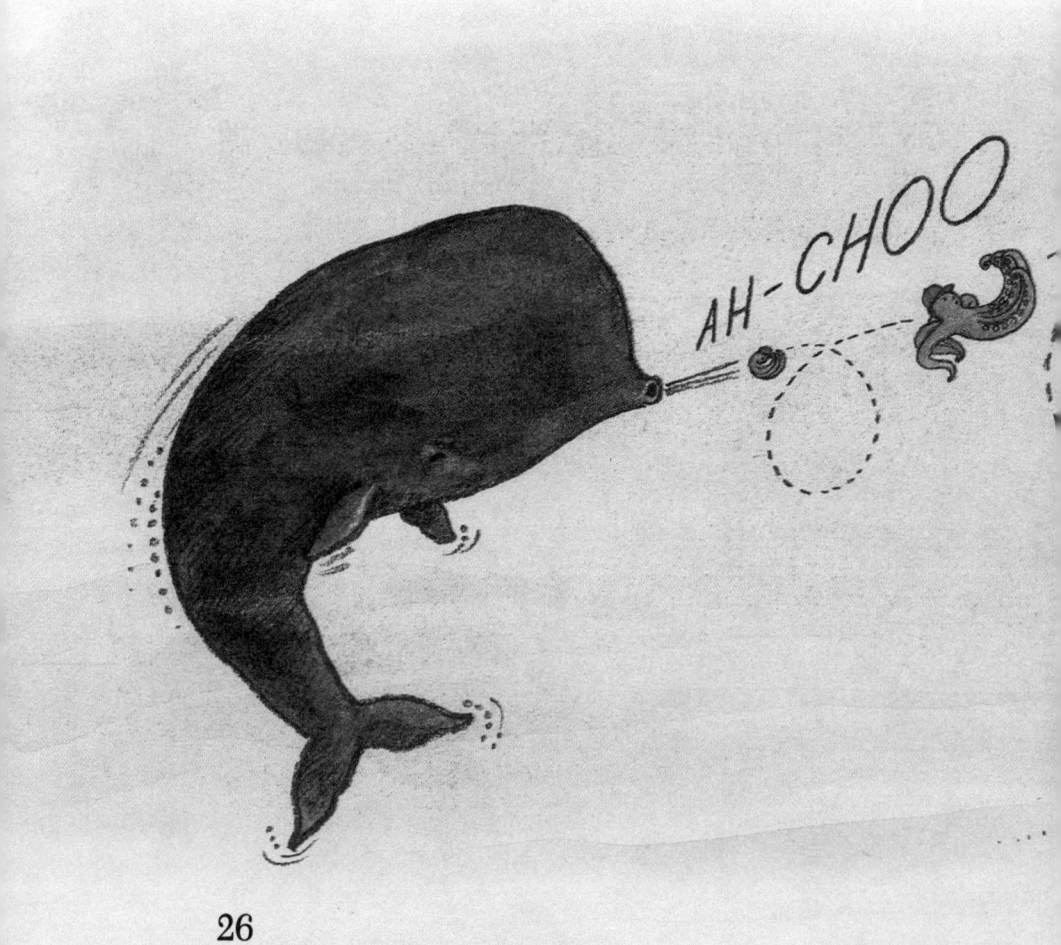

BONK! Elroy crashed into something. It was the mast pole of an old sunken ship.

Elroy grabbed onto the mast. He wrapped his tentacles around it. ZIP! Down the mast pole he slid.

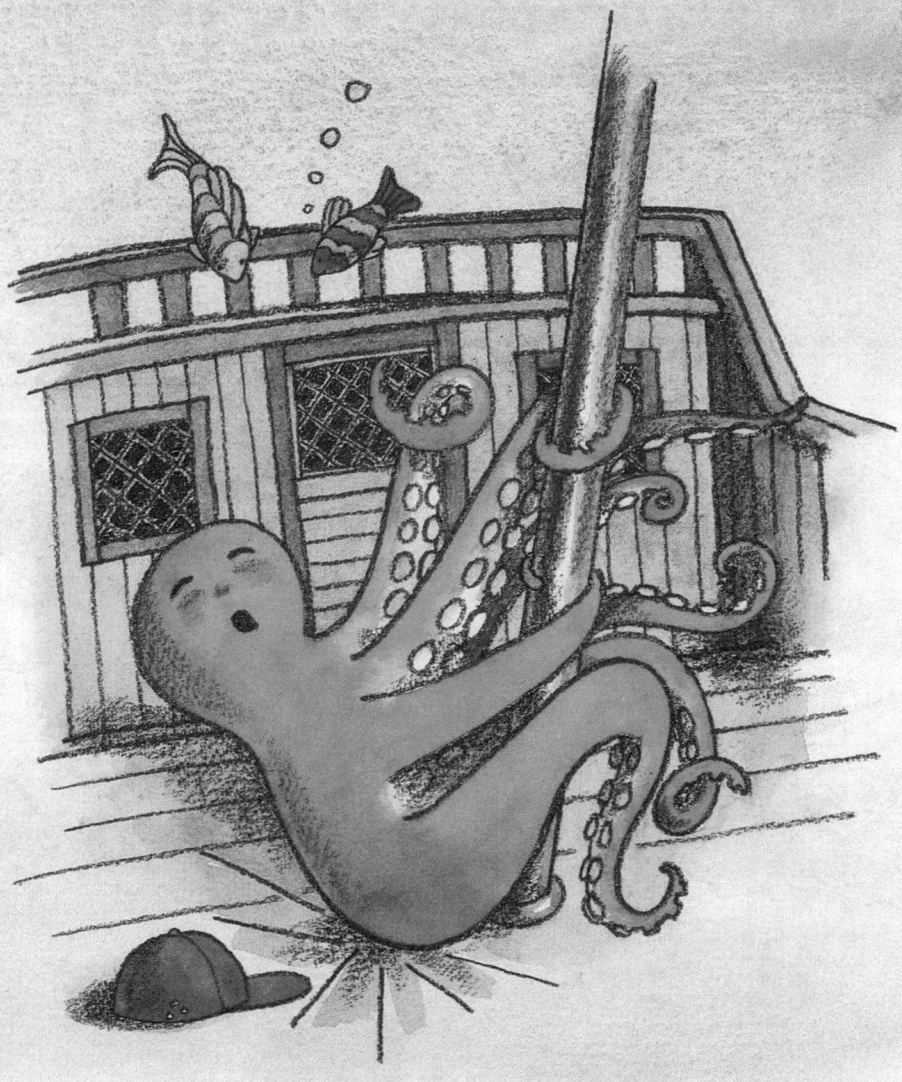

THUD! He landed on the deck!
OUCH! He landed so hard his
backside hurt.

There on the deck Elroy sat.
He was sore and dizzy. He had
nothing new to do. Poor Elroy.

Finally his head stopped spinning. He looked around. "This is an old pirate ship!" he yelled. "Exploring a sunken ship is something new to do."

Elroy began to explore. The pirate ship was spooky. It was scary. It made Elroy shake.

In an old room, Elroy found something special. It was a pirate chest. He opened the lid.

"Oh boy! A sunken treasure," cried Elroy. "Playing with pirate treasure is something new to do."

Elroy sat on the chest. He put a crown on his head. He put rings on his eight arms.
"I wonder how I look?" he asked.

A spooky voice answered.
"You look good enough to eat,"
the voice said.

"Who is that?" Elroy asked. He looked around. He saw a scary shark. The shark wanted to eat Elroy.

Elroy began to shake. Off fell the crown. Off fell the rings.

"Goodbye," said Elroy.
He squirted black octopus ink in the shark's eye. That was a special trick of his. The shark could not see Elroy.

Quickly, he swam up, up, and
away from the sunken ship.
"I want something new to do
that is not so scary," said Elroy.

Elroy sat on a big rock. What new thing could he do now? He wanted something that did not pinch. He wanted something that did not make him dizzy. He wanted something that was not scary.

"I want something new to do,"
he cried. "But what?"

"You can play with me," said
someone new. "My name is Edna.
I live here."
Edna was special. She had eight
long, wiggly arms, just like Elroy.
Edna was an octopus, too.

Elroy smiled at Edna.
"My name is Elroy," he said.
Edna smiled back at Elroy.

Elroy said, "Playing with a friend is something new to do. What can we do, friend?"

Edna answered, "We can go swimming. We can go fishing. We can go juggle clam shells."

"Let's do all of those things," said Elroy. He knew doing the same old things with a new friend could be lots and lots of fun.

And it was!